Children's Books:
One Hundred Eggs
For Henrietta

Sally Huss

ISBN: 069240015X
ISBN 13: 9780692400159

"Hurry up, girls! Keep laying those eggs. Easter is coming and we don't have nearly enough for the big hunt."

Henrietta stood inside the henhouse wringing her hands. She was in charge of the hens and she knew she was going to be short of eggs.

This Easter Sunday, unlike all of the previous Easter Sundays, Farmer Johnson had invited all of the town's children to the farm for a special Easter Egg Hunt, all one hundred of them. Henrietta had to have things ready.

"My, my, my," she fretted, as she looked at the meager number of eggs she was collecting. "Two. One. Four. Three. Two. None. No, this was not going to do." She would never reach her goal of one hundred eggs. Every child had to have an egg or it just wouldn't be Easter.

It wasn't that her chickens were lazy. They definitely were not. They were just tired and exhausted from trying to lay more eggs than usual.

"Henry," she called to the rooster, "bring more food for the girls. George, get them more water."

"Oh my, oh my," Henrietta fretted some more. "How am I going to do it? We only have two days left and we're short nearly fifty eggs!"

Henrietta had been collecting eggs for a week for the usual family Easter gathering. But then, Farmer Johnson changed plans and announced that all the town's children were invited – one hundred strong.

"Oh my, oh my," Henrietta said again as she left the henhouse, still shaking her head. "I need help, lots of help."

Earlier in the week she could have picked up eggs at the market, but they were all snapped up by now. The egg shelves were empty. Easter was a big event in this little town and everyone knew that Easter wasn't Easter without eggs.

Eggs on Easter reminded everyone how wonderful life was, that spring was beginning and new life was on the way. And every child had to have an egg; it was tradition!

One hundred eggs, one hundred eggs -- that's what she needed. One hundred eggs and she was only half way. Where would she find fifty more?

Henrietta pondered her dilemma as she sat near the duck pond. The ducks were paddling in line.

The geese were splashing each other.

The swans were gracefully gliding in circles, looking in charge of it all.

Then Henrietta thought, we are all birds of a feather, we need to stick together. "You-hoo," she called to the water birds, "I need your help!"

She continued to explain, as they swam to the edge of the pond, "In two days it will be Easter Sunday and Farmer Johnson has invited all the children in town for an Easter Egg Hunt. My chickens are doing the best they can, but we are fifty eggs short. You have feathers. You are birds like us. You lay eggs. Would you help us by laying enough eggs for the hunt?"

"Of course. Of course. We'd love to help," announced one of the swans, speaking for the whole group.

"Yes, yes. We'd love to help," piped up one of the other water birds.

"Thank you all," replied Henrietta, as she headed off to solve the next problem on her list. Eggs were one thing, but coloring them was another.

Fortunately, Farmer Johnson had rows and rows of strawberries, blueberries, raspberries and boysenberries – all perfect coloring materials. But who would be careful enough to do the dyeing?

Aha, she thought, the rabbits! Bunny rabbits have soft paws, just right for holding eggs, as long as the bunnies didn't eat the eggs in the process. Of course the eggs would be hard-boiled by the time they would be given to the rabbits to dye. But still, every egg must be handled carefully, remain whole and uncracked, and perfect for the child who would find it.

"Here, Bunny, Bunny, Bunny," called Henrietta.

Out scampered five very perky bunnies, each wondering what a chicken could want with them.

"I need your help. Farmer Johnson is having a big Easter egg party here on Sunday and we need to prepare the eggs."

"The eggs are being laid as we speak," she continued, "but they need to be colored. Could you take the berries in the berry patch, crush them and gently dye each egg?"

Proud that they had been asked to help with the festivities, the rabbits all agreed that they were on board. They were ready and willing to dye the eggs.

"Thank you, thank you," Henrietta called back to them while she headed off to solve another problem on her list.

Who would she find to hide the eggs? Who were the sneakiest animals on the farm? The cats! They knew every nook and cranny on the property. They would surely find the best hiding places.

"Here, Kitty, Kitty. Here, Kitty, Kitty," she called.

A few seconds later three multi-colored calico cats appeared.

Hardly ever are chickens and cats seen together. However, this was a desperate situation -- she needed their help.

The cats stood patiently as Henrietta explained, "Could you three cats hide one hundred dyed eggs in the middle of the night before the children arrive on Sunday morning?" She knew this was a lot to ask. She held her breath, hoping for the best.

The cats proudly said, "Yes, we could even hide two hundred eggs, if it were necessary."

"No, no," said Henrietta, very grateful that the cats wished to lend a hand -- or paw. "Thank you, thank you," she yelled, as she ran off again. "I'll be in touch."

That was it. That was the last problem to be handled on Henrietta's list. Now they just had to do it.

For the next two days, Henrietta ran from the henhouse to the duck pond to the rabbits in the field, all the while collecting, carrying, and counting eggs.

Eighty-six, eighty-seven, eighty-eight. They were getting closer. However, the hens were getting weaker, the water birds were looking paler, and the bunnies' paws were becoming stained and sore. On and on they labored.

Ninety-six, ninety-seven, ninety-eight, ninety-nine…

On the brink of hitting one hundred eggs, everyone was exhausted. Finished. Not another egg could be had from the girls in the henhouse or the birds on the pond. Not another strawberry could be found to dye another egg.

It was Saturday night and the cats were working feverishly. "Oh my, oh my," Henrietta continued her fretting. "We are one egg short and one child too many."

Drumming her head early the next morning, Henrietta tried to find a solution to her newest problem -- where could she find one more egg?

Just then from high on top an apple tree, a very tiny
hummingbird swooped down, holding the most exquisite, tiny,
golden egg in her feathered hand.

Offering it to Henrietta, she said, "I've been watching all of you working so hard to fulfill the dream of every child of having an Easter egg on Easter Sunday. I see that you are lacking one egg. I would like to do what I can to help in my small way. Here is my egg."

Gratefully, Henrietta took the egg, golden in color with a hint of blue and smaller in size than a pea, and gently placed it on a blade of grass beneath the apple tree. "My, my," thought Henrietta, "this is the most beautiful egg of all. Surely some small child will find it and love it with all of his or her heart. It is perfect."

She thanked the hummingbird, as it rose from its hovering position and disappeared into the sky.

With the rising sun on Easter Sunday, Farmer Johnson opened the gates to welcome his visitors – one hundred happy children with their Easter baskets in hand. Each ran in a different direction looking for a hidden treasure – a purple egg, a pink egg, a blue egg, a rose egg, or a green one.

As each child found an egg, he or she would help another child find theirs. The finding and helping continued until all the baskets were filled and all the eggs were discovered, all except for one – the hundredth egg!

A very little girl still had an empty basket. She wandered among the grass, searching for her egg.

From the top of the apple tree, the small hummingbird watched. She could see the little girl hunting and searching, unable to find an egg to call her own.

Then in a flash of speed, the hummingbird dove to where her egg lay gleaming on that small blade of grass.

She hovered above it, drawing attention to herself and the spot where the egg rested.

A moment later, the little girl held the very little Easter egg in her hand. It was as golden as the sun and more beautiful than the wings of the one who had laid it, the hummingbird. The little girl held it so sweetly and gently. She loved it with all her heart.

In the barnyard the Easter party continued with ice cream and cake for one and all -- that included the fine-feathered friends who had made this special Easter Sunday a day to remember.

Every child had an egg and every egg carried a wish of a bright and happy future for the one who found it!

It was a wonderful Easter – perfect in every way.

The end,
but not the end
of helping
and celebrating.

At the end of this book you will find a Certificate of Merit that may be issued to any child who promises to honor the requirements stated in the Certificate. This fine Certificate will easily fit into a 5"x7" frame, and happily suit any girl or boy who receives it!

Sally writes new books all the time. If you would like to be alerted when one of her new books is available and also when one of her books is offered FREE on Amazon, sign up for her newsletter here: http://www.sallyhuss.com/kids-books.html.

If you liked ONE HUNDRED EGGS FOR HENRIETTA, please be kind enough to post a short review on Amazon. Here is the link: http://amzn.com/B00IZ25FYQ.

About the Author/Illustrator

Sally Huss

"Bright and happy," "light and whimsical" have been the catch phrases attached to the writings and art of Sally Huss for over 30 years. Sweet images dance across all of Sally's creations, whether in the form of children's books, paintings, wallpaper, ceramics, baby bibs, purses, clothing, or her King Features syndicated newspaper panel "Happy Musings."

Sally creates children's books to uplift the lives of children and hopes you will join her in this effort by helping spread her happy messages.

Sally is a graduate of USC with a degree in Fine Art and through the years has had 26 of her own licensed art galleries throughout the world.

This certificate may be cut out, framed, and presented to any child who demonstrates her or his worthiness to receive it.

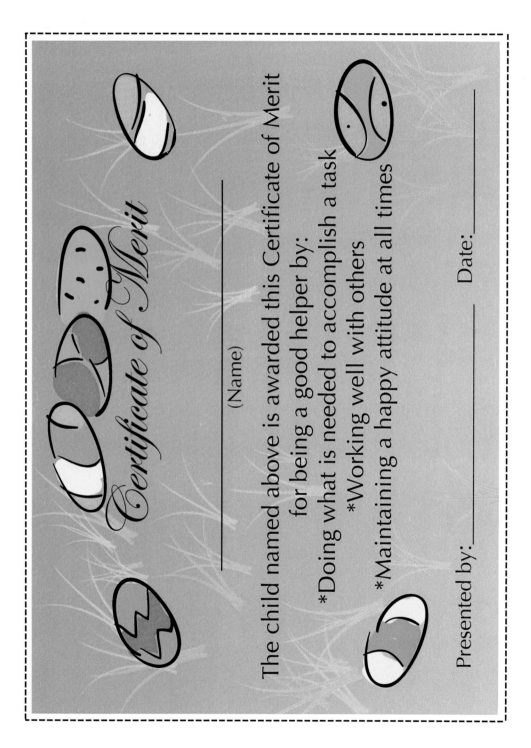

Certificate of Merit

(Name)

The child named above is awarded this Certificate of Merit for being a good helper by:

*Doing what is needed to accomplish a task
*Working well with others
*Maintaining a happy attitude at all times

Presented by: _____

Date: _____

Made in the USA
Middletown, DE
19 March 2016